I0544404

THE QUEEN'S
BEDROOM

Also by Ledru Baker, Jr.

And Be My Love
The Cheaters
Brute Madness

THE QUEEN'S BEDROOM

LEDRU BAKER JR.

CUTTING EDGE

Copyright © 1957 by Ledru Baker, Jr.

The characters and events portrayed in this book are fictitious. Any similarity
to real persons, living or dead, is coincidental and not intended by the author.
No part of this book may be reproduced, or stored in a retrieval system,
or transmitted in any form or by any means, electronic, mechanical,
photocopying, recording, or otherwise, without express written permission
of the publisher.

This was originally published in the August 1957 issue of *Tales of the Frightened*.

ISBN-13: 978-1-952138-81-2

Published by
Cutting Edge Books
PO Box 8212
Calabasas, CA 91372
www.cuttingedgebooks.com

THE QUEEN'S
BEDROOM

BY LEDRU BAKER, JR.

YOU take a pair of scales, you can pick them up at any bazaar in Cairo, and put the chance for fame and riches on one side. Then you balance them with the possibility of death on the other. Nine times out of ten, if you are like me, you will tip them just a little in favor of the first choice.

It isn't cold down here, just sort of damp. I am alone in a tomb near Cairo, Egypt, some ninety feet under the hard desert rock. Memories are flooding back at me across the darkness, dancing jerkily in tune with the flickering candle. Behind me, Queen Hetepheres lies in state. I am the only one who knows of her presence. One other man knew, but he is dead too. Notice how I said "Too?"

Funny how this hits you. Once you know you are dying, and just as soon as you get used to the idea, it doesn't hurt much. It's just a little like waiting for an interview. Here I am, you might say, in the ante-chamber of eternity, waiting for my appointment. Soon, a great shining light, a jackal-headed God or maybe a multi-headed being will come into the tomb to escort me away. Maybe I know too much about too many religions and not enough about any single one. I cannot believe, and at this moment, sincerely wish that I could.

If it hadn't been for one or two small, connected events, I wouldn't be here now; I would be in my room a bare mile away in the Mena House Hotel, where I was when the old man entered my life.

There was a light rapping at the door, and I said "Come in," in French, thinking it was the house servant. The door opened slowly and like a gnome from an ancient woodcut, a face peeked around at me.

"Mr. Andrews?" he said. His voice was high and arid like the plains of the Lybian desert.

I arose and walked toward him. "That's right. Rolly Andrews," I admitted. "'What brings an American to Cairo in this season?" A fly buzzed onto his forehead and he ignored it like a native.

He grinned toothily. "I'm Dr. Barkley. M. Durand of the National Museum told me a fellow American was staying here. Welcome to Egypt, sir."

My wheels were turning slowly, and I must have looked puzzled, because he added, "I should have said—a brother archeologist." When he shook my hand, his grasp was surprisingly strong.

And then it clicked. Sure, Dr. David Barkley, a pretty famous old boy who was highly thought of in grave-digging circles. I invited him to sit down; good contacts never hurt any man. He smiled his way out onto my terrace and eased himself into a chair. Across the road and on the plateau the pyramids waited for the setting sun and the start of another night of silence.

When I sat down facing him, he said, "I understand from M. Durand that you are here on a buying expedition, sir."

I nodded, afraid I was in for a gentle lecture. "That's right. Old 'Ink For Blood' wants a few mummys for the Egyptian Room in his museum."

"What was his name?" he asked. "Ink For ..."

"... Blood. Roger Simpson—he owns the World News Service. He's got more money than he can hide from the Treasury Department, so he's investing a little of it in culture for us peasants. He has men all over the world, and I'm here doing my bit."

"I see." The old man leaned forward and chuckled. "I guess Egypt can stand the loss of a few mummys. The people need money badly, and I'm glad your Mr. Ink For Blood is willing to help us. Just leave the pyramids, that's all we ask."

I laughed heartily at that. Laughs are fun once you get into the spirit of things. They don't cost anything, and sometimes they pay off pretty good odds. The old boy must have been there close to an hour, bleating about the past. For a while it was interesting; but when, for the third time, he made a round trip and started back on the 1928 Lower Nile Expedition, I was suddenly very tired of the whole thing and wished I had never opened the door. I gently steered the talk into a blind alley. He looked confused, shook his head uncertainly and fished in his pocket for a huge watch.

"I didn't realize it was so late!" he said. "Would you join me for dinner, Rolly?"

We were in the David-Rolly stage by that time. I don't know why I agreed unless it was his apparent loneliness. To take the edge off an unpromising evening I had three drinks at the bar and about seven o'clock went back to the dining room. I stood beneath the arches and looked around. His wasted, hunched body was sitting at a table across the room. A girl sat opposite him, and I unconsciously pulled my tie straighter.

The girl's back was to me, and as Barkley arose she half turned to face me. She was about twenty-five and even though she was seated, it was easy to tell she was tall and slender. She was wearing a bright, red dress that matched her crimson lips perfectly. Her hair was dark and reached down to touch her white, bare shoulders. She looked into my eyes and must have read something special in them, because she took a deep, nervous breath, then smiled.

Barkley introduced us and I sat down in the vacant chair next to her. She was his daughter, and her name was Janice. That night they could have served me fried scarabs, garnished with reeds from the Nile and I would have paid the check without a grumble. After we ate I cast, rebaited and cast again. Each time she wriggled off the hook, but her vivid eyes kept asking for more, so I kept on trying for a strike.

Finally she laughed and leaned forward. I had trouble keeping my eyes from the deep "V" of her breasts, and her secret smile told me she realized as much. "Now, wait a minute, Rolly," she said. "Didn't anyone tell you that approach went out with the bustle?"

Old man Barkley jumped, for the first time seeming to hear our banter. "Approach—bustle! What a thing to say to Mr. Andrews, my dear!"

He was still clucking when she smiled across at him. "Dad, don't be that way! I was just explaining to Rolly how time changes all things—from bait to lines. He understands, don't you, Rolly?"

The old man looked at me and smiled uncertainly. "I just don't know what happened to the little girl I sent to finishing school ten years ago. Why when she ..."

Janice interrupted him gently. "Believe me, dad, they nearly *did* finish me. That's why I ran away and got on my own. I've been modeling for some of the women's magazines," she explained to me.

I started to tell her that she was a damned sight better looking than most of the models I had seen in those smart-set magazines, but I didn't. Instead, I said to him, "I think Janice is trying to say that the school was—ah, in danger of squaring the circle, David. Right?" I asked the girl.

Her eyes swept over mine, doing a re-appraising job. "Bless you," she smiled. "I see that shovels aren't the only things you dig with."

Her leg moved slowly until it touched mine. It might have been an accident, but it wasn't. Barkley resumed his brooding silence, his mind probably back on the 1928 expedition. The orchestra segued into a smoky tango, and red-fezed Egyptian waiters glided silently around the room, their lips curled in smiles, but their eyes as expressionless as those of the great sphinx. Barkley seemed to doze, and once his head fell forward sharply onto his breast. I wished to heaven he would go to bed and dream whatever ancient grave diggers dream when they sleep. No one spoke for several minutes and the silence became oppressive.

The girl's eyes locked with mine, nakedly and boldly. Finally she shook her head and said, "Have you ever been to Egypt before?"

At that word, the old man's head jerked erect. She smiled and reached for his hand. She liked her father more than a little, and I knew it wouldn't hurt me to patronize him just a bit.

I shook my head. "No, but your father's book on the Old Kingdom has been a great help. In fact, part of my thesis was based on it." The old man had written a book—I had never read it.

He blossomed like a century plant. "Thank you. That book was my life's work, but I know that a lot is lacking." He looked at Janice, then at me again. "That is why I am back in Egypt at this late date."

I wasn't interested, just wanted him to go to bed. But I said, "More research, sir?"

He thought a long second and finally said, "Not exactly. You know of Queen Hetepheres, I imagine."

"Old Cheops mother, wasn't she?"

"Yes." He looked as if he wanted to pat me on the head and give me a hundred percent for the day. "As you probably know, her tomb is located near here. In my opinion, whatever it may be worth, the place has never been fully explored. With my friend Durand's permission, I have reopened it."

He leaned forward, and his eyes were as bright as a desert bird's. "If I am right this will make history second only to the Rosetta Stone. There is an unexplained gap in Egyptian history that ends with the death of Cheops and his mother, to take up again only after thirty years."

I couldn't see what was so damned important about a thirty-year gap in a five-thousand year old history, but it was getting the old boy hopped up, so I nodded. His hand grasped mine, it was like a claw, and the strength in his fingers made me wince. I lit a cigarette, my mind whirling, too many ideas trying to crash into it.

"I'm very happy for you, David," I said. "Your name will never be forgotten."

He leaned across the table, and his fingers dug into the white cloth. "I am not young like I was forty years ago. I need a young man to work with me—to help me. From the very first minute I saw you, I liked you, probably because you were polite and listened to an old man talking about something that happened when you were still a baby. Would you consider helping me, boy?"

That was probably what I should have wanted the most, but it didn't listen good. Who remembers the man who wields the shovel? The old man would get the full loaf of glory, and I would be lucky to grab the crust. You can't spread much butter on one of them. I glanced at Janice, but her eyes turned to look at the orchestra, and her leg moved away, leaving mine suddenly lonesome. Right then I knew there was only one thing to say:

"I'll be happy to work with you, David."

The girl turned back to me, her lips softened, and they seemed to be saying, "Thanks. Thanks for helping an old man make his last dream come true." Barkley pushed back the chair and arose. When we shook hands, I made mine just a little stronger than I should have. But I knew he was from the old school whose graduates can read a man's character by the strength of his hand grasp. I started to help Janice from her chair, but I wanted her to stay with me as much as I wanted to take my next breath.

He must have read my thoughts, then dug back into the dusty pages of his youth. "No!" he protested. "You two stay here as long as you like and enjoy youth while you can. I will see you in the morning."

He tottered away, and I sat down next to Janice. There were lots of things to say to her, but when she waited for me to speak, there was nothing I could think of to say.

She finally broke the charged silence. "Rolly, take care of dad. He really shouldn't be here—his heart."

"I'll watch him like a hawk." My hand reached over and covered hers. Suddenly as if a falling pillar had struck me, I knew why I had been intrigued the moment I first looked at her. In the Cairo museum they had a statuette of her, only it must have been made in a previous life. From her hair and cheeks and lips right down to her smooth neck she was the total likeness of Queen Tewosret.

I was trying to phrase the compliment in the right way when she suddenly said, "Are you married, Rolly?"

"If I had a wife, would I be sitting here with you?" I said. "No, I never tried it. I couldn't ask any woman to share my life. One year in New York, the next in Central America. From opening a tomb in Assyria on Christmas Day to God knows what on Washington's Birthday."

"You don't like your work," she stated.

"Not especially—anymore. But I'm thirty-two, and I don't know anything else."

"Why did you ever start it?"

"I wish I knew. I liked to read books on things like your father was just talking about, and naturally I took a few courses in archeology in college. The first thing I knew, I had changed my Major from Business Administration to Archeology."

She smiled faintly. "From an advertising executive to a grave robber in one easy chat with the dean," she mused. "I've often wondered why dad made it his life's work. He's world-famous, but I doubt if he has five-thousand dollars in the bank."

"Was your mother happy with him?"

"My mother died shortly after I was born, but I've read some of her letters to my father." The girl looked into the darkness. "No," she said flatly. "My mother wasn't happy. There was no reason for her to be. Father was gone nearly all the year. And after mother died, I lived with relatives here and there and everywhere. I would never put up with what my mother did."

While she was speaking, I had been looking at my hands. They were already curling into the permanent shapes of those of a shovel holder. I shook my head, then said, "Have you been to the formal gardens yet?"

"I've seen them from my window. They are very lovely."

"Let me show them to you—now."

I ground out the cigarette and held my breath. She hesitated, but I don't believe she was being coy. She wasn't yet sure of her feelings for me, and she knew what would happen when we were alone. Finally she arose, and her hair brushed against my face; it smelled purple. As we turned toward the arches I lightly took her arm. It was there, and somehow it was not. It was like touching heaven, or maybe a dream. If you have ever loved, you understand; if you have not, you never will.

We descended the stairway into the night. Great white clouds were massing overhead for their march over the desert; and behind them the sky was black, creating a massive backdrop for the gardens. For the first time in my life I began to feel the power of nature and realized that there were things which could not be purchased on the open market.

Neither of us spoke as we walked through the gardens. When we reached the outer edge we stood looking up at the great pyramid of Cheops which lay across the road and up a winding path. I took her arm again and we moved toward the thing. Resembling a gigantic symphony, Cheops rose before us, shimmering in the pale darkness. For a long time we stood beneath the great folly, then I turned to her.

I started to speak, but her mouth was waiting for mine, her lips parted, her eyes half-closed. I think maybe I got a little of her soul in that kiss, but it was an even trade. Her body pressed against mine and her fingers dug into my back. When the long kiss was over, she looked up at me.

"I have never been kissed like that before," she said honestly.

That was all she said, but I knew she was my woman. I took her hand in mine and led her back to the hotel.

Hours later we were still in my room. She kissed me softly and spoke. "It's very late. I must be leaving."

She arose, took my arm and led me to the open window. We stood, looking over at old Cheops who still reared against the sky and was now pinned down to the earth by sharp, twinkling stars.

When she finally left, I sat alone in the darkness. Before tonight, whenever anything was wanted there had been only one logical course for me to follow: Go out and get it, or get the old face ground into the dirt, trying. Time after time my feet had almost touched those elusive steps that lead to fame and riches. But each time someone just a little more clever than I had reached out, pulled me back and vaulted over my shoulders. More than once it had been the very man whom I had tried to outsmart.

And now once again, the likely passage to success, via the Barkley route, was in my hands. I knew I would not spoil things by taking a trip at her father's expense. But would I? How would I act if the chance rose before me?

It was barely dawn when the phone rang. I was instantly awake, and in the time it took my hand to lift the receiver, my mind had relived the previous day right down to the last kiss. Barkley's voice rustled dryly over the phone.

"Rolly—it's David. How are you, boy?"

I leaned back on the bed. "Fine, I was already up. Are you ready to start?"

"Anytime. I'll meet you after you have eaten. Say—an hour from now in the lobby?"

He was waiting for me in the main hall half an hour or so later. He was an almost ludicrous sight in his faded khaki clothes and over-sized pith helmet. Strapped about his waist was a canteen and small pack of miscellaneous items. When he saw me he slung a pack of tools over his bent shoulders and waved. He was surrounded by a rabid group of natives and was having trouble shooing them away. This morning he seemed younger, more alert, and I felt kindly toward him, realizing that this was what he lived for.

Pushing my way through the circle of native servants, I lifted the pack from his shoulders. "I see you're ready for the battle," I smiled.

"If I can get rid of my friends here," he nodded. He rattled off a few decisive words, his blue eyes sparkling gently as he cursed them away. They grinned and opened a path for us.

We left the hotel grounds, taking the same route Janice and I had walked the night before. But the red sun was clearing the memories away, heartlessly sweeping them into the sand. Old Cheops was merely a pile of stones, prosaic in his ancient calm. We trudged onto the rise and gradually the Sphinx came into view.

"There's something for you," Barkley said. "For ages we humans have been trying to solve his riddle, and the answer is there for everyone to see. He's just an old fellow who has turned to stone and is now very tired. He is waiting patiently for the end of the world. If he has a spirit, it will be set free then at that moment."

He looked up at me and smiled a little guiltily. He ducked his head and added, "… Just an old man making up daydreams. I really don't believe any of it."

We took off on a tangent across the sands, passing near to the Temple of the Dead, cut left over a rocky plateau, then were suddenly at our destination. The steel grating had been unlocked by Durand of the museum, and the large, flat rocks had been pushed away, leaving a gaping hole at our feet. Some ninety feet down was the floor of the tomb.

In my travels I had been in many tombs, had inhaled the special odor they always emit, and usually felt a certain exhilaration, probably because I was alive in the presence of death. But this place was different. It was damp, and its smell hit my nostrils hard like an actual impact from the unknown. I had never been an imaginative person, but my skin seemed to crawl, and the hair rose on my neck as I tried to fight off a feeling of stark terror.

A scraping noise behind my back made me wheel about. It sounded for all the world like some walled-up spirit fighting for its freedom. Barkley was scraping the floor with his shovel. Until he had switched on the flashlight, the only light was that which filtered dustily down the shaft. He placed the shovel against the stone coffin in the center of the chamber, then without speaking focused the light on the far wall. His aim was accurate and the light remained steady on one spot as we walked across the room.

"This is what we came to see, boy. This is it!"

Inscriptions that once living hands had painted onto the dead rock huddled together. Words of death and resurrection made their silent, pleading way around the walls of the tomb. Everything on the positive side of the ledger that could be said about Queen Hetepheres was here painted by slave hands. We made our way around the tomb, Barkley explaining as we walked, his voice echoing about the chamber.

"The inscriptions stop at this point. Now, look closely; the God Osiris was being addressed, and they would have never insulted him unless..." His eyes looked into mine, and they had the snap of a twenty-year old boy's. "Nothing but some major change could have caused the prayers."

"What do you think it was?" I asked. My voice was harsh and unnatural in its hollow tone. The old grasping Rolly Andrews was returning, and my fingers clenched tightly to fight off his approach.

The old man shook his head. "I don't know, it has always been a major puzzle. It might have been an invasion, or uprising. Maybe we will find the answer today."

"But what about the coffin in the center of the room?" I asked him.

The light swept toward the empty case. It was eight feet long, less than three feet high and about that wide. "That's just it," Barkley said. "Her body was never found, and there is no evidence of robbers being here—before us," he added with a little smile.

"But the tomb was searched thoroughly, wasn't it?" I pointed to several drill holes in the wall where men had probed for hidden chambers.

Barkley shook his head. "I have studied all the reports since the tomb was discovered. It has been searched well—except one place." The light flashed over the coffin, then down to its base. "*There!*"

"You mean—under it?" I gasped.

"Exactly," he replied calmly.

I wondered how the old man expected to move the heavy stone thing, and he must have read my thoughts, because he smiled happily. "You'll see that the old man came prepared, Rolly." He reached deep into the sack and pulled out several wedges, three steel bars about four feet in length and a small hydraulic jack. As he threaded the bars together he said rather smugly, "We'll let the laws of nature help us a bit."

I could not help but grin at him. Minutes later we had the jack pressed against the base of the coffin and the bars against the near wall. I was preparing to operate the handle when Barkley lay a gentle hand on my shoulder.

"I know you want to be helpful, but would you mind? I mean—this will be the last great thing of my life—*if* we find what I hope we will. Do you understand?" he almost pleaded.

"Of course, go ahead, sir."

He grabbed for the handle and started pumping furiously. The coffin, having been rooted for God knows how many centuries seemed tied to the earth. Sweat dripped from the old man's face as he pumped more slowly. I was about to take over the job when the coffin started across the floor. Thirty minutes later it had moved four feet and Barkley examined the spot where it had rested. He brushed away dirt and sand which someone had scattered so many eras past and suddenly shouted. He pointed down with a trembling finger.

"The *Ka*—the soul!"

In the black slate of the floor was carved the symbol of the genius that lived in her body during life. Barkley screamed happily and leapt up to grab the crowbar. I felt a little like crying, because there was no doubt that he had made a discovery. I had wanted to return empty-handed to the hotel, meet Janice for dinner and have life flow on smoothly from that point.

I watched him pry up one of the stones, saw his mouth drop open and a scream of pain pass his lips. I barely managed to catch him before his head hit the coffin. I lowered him gently to the floor, and when I bent over him I seemed to hear the words of Janice as a pleading whisper—*Rolly, take care of dad. He isn't well.*

David Barkley, world-famous archeologist lay moaning at my feet, his withered body appearing to wither as he writhed in pain. I felt his pulse; it was an irregular thing, skipping beats, coming back a little stronger, then fading away, each time a bit weaker. His lips moved wordlessly, but at last he managed to gasp:

"Medicine—coat pocket. Help me!"

I thrust my hand into the left pocket first, then quickly over to the right before finding the small bottle. My fingers curled over it and I looked down at the man. His large eyes begged me for life, and I pitied him at first. But through contact with the bottle, I suddenly felt a great strength. Like a small, fluttering bird in my hand, I held the power of life or death over this wasted thing. My thoughts narrowed down into one channel as I stared into his eyes.

He must have read my thoughts, because his talon-like fingers clutched at mine and he screeched, "Help me, boy!"

I withdrew my hand, hiding the vial in my fist. "I am sorry, there is nothing I can do. The medicine is not there."

His hand jerked back and his head fell to one side then rolled back to stare at me. My fingers remained on his pulse, feeling him slowly die. It took him several minutes, and his sorrowful eyes never left mine. The pulse speeded up one final time, then stopped. I placed the medicine in the pocket nearest to me, straightened out the old man's corpse and stood up.

As in the past, the tide of affairs had been turned to my advantage, with one difference. I knew this time nothing could stand in my way. I became the old methodical Rolly Andrews as I pried up the flat stone and flashed the light into a chamber some eight feet deep.

I saw two things through the narrow opening. The mummy case of the queen and an alabaster casket, but it was enough. Half an hour later the coffin was in place, and I saluted the floor beneath it. "Get caught up on your sleep, because I'll be back later."

It had taken more than a little will power to keep from entering the chamber, but I knew it must wait. I had to have time to view the scene in leisure, removing certain items for private sale before telling the scientific world about the discovery. Fame can be pretty wonderful, but there is no percentage in walking around as a tattered celebrity.

I left the tomb and climbed into the stabbing Egyptian heat. The first heat waves were beginning their undulating dance over the sands. To the south the Sphinx settled on its haunches to live through another day. A distance away three people were making their way up the terraced sides of old Cheops while three eternal camels knelt patiently at the base. A few minutes later I had walked down the road and entered the cool lobby of the Mena House. I had just turned toward the stairs when Janice ran across the room and called to me.

"Rolly, what's wrong?" she cried. I looked down at her without speaking. She was clutching at me, fear staining her face. "Where is he?" she begged.

I took her arm and was not acting when I said, "I am sorry, Janice. David—passed away in the tomb."

No, I wished at that moment that somehow the chance to relive the last hour might be given me. In a low voice that was barely audible she said:

"His medicine, it was in his pocket."

People were beginning to watch us as I led her to a divan by the broad window. I held her hands in mine and said, "I didn't know, Janice. But it wouldn't have made any difference. He died immediately after the attack. He said just two words as I was holding him. 'Carry on', he said. Then he—died."

As I held her in my arms, stroking her hair, a tender feeling replaced the burning desire of last night. She was a girl who needed help—help from the man who had let her father die.

"I loved him so, Rolly," she said quietly. "He was all I cared about until..." She closed her eyes. "Help me, I don't know what to do now."

"Leave everything to me," I nodded. "He was my friend—and I want to help."

Without taking her head from my shoulder she asked me the question I most dreaded to hear, yet which I knew must come eventually. "Was there anything down in that awful place, Rolly?"

I patted her shoulder. "We'll talk about it later, dear."

She looked up at me. "Somehow it wouldn't seem so bad if you had discovered something. I mean, Egypt was his life and ..."

"Of course. And now I'm going to take you to your room."

"What will you do about him?"

"Durand will help me. I'll go into town at once."

"Whatever you say," she said in a tired, dry voice. "You know best, Rolly."

I left her in her room and hurried down the hall. Deep in my stomach there was an actual physical sickness, but once outside in the sunlight the feeling left me, and I squared my shoulders to face the most important task of all—convincing Durand of my friendship with David, and above all, of my sincerity. When he first heard of my mission to Egypt which had been approved by the new government, he had been rather doubtful of me, and now I must force him to believe in me. So very much depended upon it.

He arose as I entered his office. "Ah—M. Andrews," he said in precise English. "How are you this day?"

He chose his words carefully as if he were picking his way over uncertain ground. He motioned to a chair, but I decided to remain standing. With the jolt I was about to deliver him, it would look better if I were on my feet.

I answered him in his native French. "M. Durand, I have unpleasant news. Doctor Barkley is dead!"

He raised his eyebrows, drew them together, then sank into his chair and commenced drumming his fingers on the desk top. His eyes looked me over closely, then he said, "How did it happen, please?"

"We were in the tomb ..."

His eyebrows danced apart, then met violently. "We .. ?" he murmured.

Here it is, Rolly. Play it right. "We," I emphasized. "I was working in conjunction with David at his request." My mentioning Barkley by his first name got him, and he moved restlessly in his chair.

"I see," he said quietly. "When Doctor Barkley asked for permission to re-open the tomb, I did not realize he was acquainted with you. In fact—quite the contrary."

When he motioned me to a seat again, I sat down, leaning toward him. "I met David and his daughter at the hotel. He and

I took an immediate liking to each other. He finally asked me to help him—to supply the muscle power, you might say."

I paused, then said, "He asked me to carry on—in the name of science, and Egypt."

It was his move, and I prayed that I could anticipate it and move my knight to a better position.

Spreading his fingers out before him, he regarded them thoughtfully, then said, "This is all confusing. I caused the tomb to be re-opened for David Barkley because he is—was a true friend of Egypt as well as a personal friend of mine. This is very irregular."

I pulled the chair closer to his desk and sat facing the man who had achieved a terrific importance in my life. My voice was very sincere as I said, "As a promise I made to a dying man, I want to continue. He told me what he hoped to do. Monsieur, above anything else in the world, I want to keep that promise."

"But what about your buying expedition?"

"Both you and I know that is not true science. M. Durand, I hated it, but, frankly, I had to eat, and not even in your wonderful Egypt do they give food away for nothing. It may interest you that what happened today has changed my mind completely, and I am withdrawing from my buying—expedition."

The man looked at me with new interest. His eyes were more friendly, and his mind was evidently correcting its first impression of me. For God knows how long, he sat caressing a miniature sphinx that crouched on the desk. Then with a quick gesture he shoved it away from himself and arose.

He extended his hand. "As you wish," he said quietly. "You have my permission. The facilities of the museum and my humble assistance shall be yours at any time you wish to use them."

"Thank you, sir. Now about David."

"Ah, yes. Will you go with me?"

"Of course. Are you ready?" He said he was, and an hour later we had removed David's body from the tomb and returned to town. I left Durand looking down at his friend's body, left the refrigerated room and walked outside.

I hailed a gharry and relaxed against the hot leather seat. I closed my eyes and for the first time in hours, permitted myself to relax. The bent back of the native driver swayed sleepily over the reins, and the ever-present, hurrying citizens constantly crisscrossed their ways across the streets.

The hot copper sun had passed the top of the sky and was starting its long glide toward the the desert. The birds of prey circled over the city as they had done from the moment of its founding, ever-hopeful for full bellies, praying for mass death so they could feast. The white-clad figures, mingling with the smartly-dressed Europeans, the horse-drawn gharries fighting with the limousines, the new constantly vying with the old combined to make the city the best one in the world in which to study contrasts.

I discharged the driver in front of the Continental Savoy and entered the cool lobby. As badly as I wanted to see Janice, I knew it would be better if I waited until later in the day. After several drinks and an excellent meal, I emerged with my plans made. They were strong, yet sufficiently elastic to shape themselves to any sudden twist in events.

It was dusk; the muezzins had finished their prayers, the Faithful had arisen from the ground, gathered their robes closely about themselves and disappeared into the countless narrow, dark streets. Fifteen minutes later, I was back at the Mena House. A necklace in the window of the hotel gift shop had caught my eye, and after a few minutes of haggling with the friendly thief behind the counter, I left with it my pocket.

She was dressed in something green that clung to her body, highlighting the youth that she carried so very proudly. I pulled her into my arms, her eyes closed and she held me closely.

"M. Durand called," she finally said.

"I thought he would. I was with him most of the afternoon."

"Was there anything in the tomb?" she asked.

I looked at the wall, then into her eyes. My own were open and honest when I said, "I can't be sure, but for his sake, I hope there is. It would have meant a lot to him."

I reached into my pocket and pulled out the necklace which was modeled after a treasure of the Middle Kingdom. When I clasped it about her neck, she smiled gratefully and kissed me. The next morning we ate together. Neither of us spoke much until we were smoking and sipping our strong coffee. She finally told me that Durand had called and asked for permission to bury her father in the museum ground. She wanted to know what I thought of it.

"It would be a great honor," I said. "As far as I know, only one or two other men have ever been buried there. If I were you—I would agree."

"When are you going down into the—place?" she asked.

"Perhaps tomorrow," I told her. "I want to spend today with you. What would you like to do?"

"I don't know, it doesn't matter. Anything that will keep me from thinking about father's death. I don't want to be alone, Rolly."

"Have you ever seen the Temple of the Dead?"

"No. Where is it?"

"Less than a mile from here. Would you like to see it?"

"It would be nice, I think. What should I wear?"

"Anything, but include hiking boots. I don't want any scorpions getting familiar with your legs."

We left the hotel ground hand in hand. Neither of us spoke until we reached the base of old Cheops. Then she rubbed her smooth cheek against mine and said, "Do you remember?"

"I'll never forget," I promised. "It's a part of me."

"I hope you mean it," she whispered. "I don't know how many women there were before me, and I really don't care—very much. Just as long as I'm the last one."

I kissed her softly and tried to shrug off the feeling that I was holding a girl in my arms whose father had died in my presence, and with my help. Then I made myself remember that the past was dead and would soon be buried, and the future was bright with promise of fame, money and love. For even though David Barkley's name would be remembered, the fame is for the man who is there and ready to receive it.

I would see to it that her father would not be forgotten, it was the least I could do. But I would be the one who would be photographed and interviewed, and the least that could possibly come out of it would be a full professorship at a first-rate American college.

We walked past the Sphinx and turned toward the temple. A ramp, once well-defined and polished leads down from the second of the great pyramids in a gentle slope. Here, in alabaster crypts were reverently placed the bodies of the translators of the creed of *Ra*. Through fruitful and sterile times, wars and famines, these were the true rulers of Egypt.

Monarchs and their dynasties danced and swayed in the winds of their incantations, for through them Gods spoke, destinies of nations shifted, men rose and fell, always to the same tune of fear.

I led Janice into the temple and proudly showed her through it. As we emerged into the bright sun from one of the crypts, the sand whispered beneath our feet. The pillars and great stones that had once held up the roof, criss-crossed their oblique shadows on the alabaster floor. We leaned against one of the pillars and looked upward at the blue, cloudless sky.

Whispering footsteps rustling across the floor of the temple made me turn with a frown. The intruder, an ancient person, shuffled toward us slowly. Janice turned and looked uncertainly at the old man who might have been any age; what is a guess worth? He might have been the spirit of one of the priests. The wrinkles which time had eroded upon his face appeared to expose his soul. He stopped within a foot of us, stared up at me for some reason, then spoke.

"The future, *Effendi?* In the sands of the temple I will tell it for you!"

The spell which his sudden appearance had created was broken. Instead of an ancient priest, he was another of the myriad of grasping Egyptians who squeezed a living from the purses of tourists. I looked down at Janice and smiled.

"Your fortune, *Madamoiselle?*" I mimicked.

"Mais oui, Monsieur, certainment," she replied.

The eyes of the old man lowered, and he motioned us toward the extreme side of the temple floor. He squatted in Egyptian fashion and gestured for me to take a place opposite to him. As I knelt down he commenced an ancient ritual. With a long, thin finger, he drew a large rectangle in the sand of the floor, cut it into four smaller ones, and closed his eyes.

In the upper left section, his fingers started tracing lines, then he suddenly announced, "You are foreign to this land. You come from across the seas."

I shrugged. "And you are Egyptian. You come from across the Nile."

He looked at me with no evidence of emotion. "I tell only what the sands say, *Effendi.*" His fingers drew more whorls, the sand scattering into tiny ridges. "You are in love," he said quietly.

I looked up at Janice who was smiling down at me. "You are correct, Wise One. Continue," I said.

His finger again patterned the sand; then as I watched his eyes, they seemed to withdraw and become nothing more than slits. His voice was low, but it echoed through the temples like a deep, tolling bell.

"You search for something, *Effendi.* It is not clear—ah, but yes, it brightens. I am allowed to know it is fame that you seek." He paused, then his voice became so low I had to strain to hear it. "You want it badly, but—even as you seek it, you fear it is not for you!"

This time I neither shrugged nor looked up at Janice, for I was afraid of what my eyes would show.

He progressed to the second square, and my nervous eyes followed his finger like a sparrow watches the circling approach of a hawk. "In the search, the sands tell me that you will lose something to find something else. I know not what it is, for the sands are quiet. But they do say that you—you…" He trailed off as his finger painted a mad pattern in the sand before suddenly stopping. His puzzled eyes were intent upon the drawing which had been created before him. Finally he unwillingly looked at me.

"Well, the sands say what?" I said impatiently.

He arose slowly, almost regally. "The telling is over, *Effendi*. There is no more."

My mouth sagged. "…What of the rest? There are still two squares left. I *demand* that you finish what you left undone!"

"I have left nothing undone, as I have started nothing," he said calmly. "What has been written here was started long before your birth. *Kismet*. And the results of them will live long after you have been forgotten."

"What did you start to tell me before you stopped? Do you want more money than you have earned?" I shouted.

His voice was very soft as he said, "But—do you really want to know? It would perhaps be better if you never heard."

"Yes! I *really* want to know!"

He straightened up and moved a step back. "Then I will tell you, but it is futile to speak of it. The sands have written that—that unless their pattern is changed, you will lose that which is most dear to you, and it is not mortal man who can change what has been written in Time. You search for Fame, *Effendi*, and for a moment in your life, you will seem to have it in your hands. But it will not be yours to keep."

"Why?" I croaked.

"I think, American, that you will be dead!"

Janice threw a hand across her horrified face and screamed. I was infuriated and whipped a pound note from my wallet, thrusting it into the old man's face.

He ignored it and said, "There is no more to be written by the sands; your life has been lived."

The money dropped from my trembling fingers and fluttered to the ground. His eyes looked deeply into mine, and I wheeled away to face the wall. As an uncertain fear came over me, I heard his footsteps fade slowly away. I turned back and looked down at the design. The money lay where it had fallen, a symbol on the ruins of my life. I looked at Janice, recalling her presence. Her own eyes were strange and fearful, searching my face as the old man had done. She shook her head, and her hands flew to her face.

"You *do* want it!" she screamed. "You do, I can see it! You want it, and you are afraid the old man spoke the truth!"

She spun around, running from the place. I raised my hand, then let it fall to my side as she sped in the path of the seer. Then I was completely alone, shut away from all the world by the thick walls of the temple. I knelt on my knees and stared intently at what Time had written for the old man. Well-defined lines with an orderly precision about them had been drawn in the first square, converging on one spot, something like a winding stairway leading to a tower. The second one started out in a similar manner, then the pattern lost its meaning in a jumble of chaotic drawings with no sane meaning—unless Death itself is a meaning.

Very slowly I gathered the sand he had used into a small cone, gently patting it into shape, then swept my hand down in an arc, obliterating all signs. The sand scattered and fell unnoticed and the spell was broken. The old man's prophecy was dead; it had never been. It was all a dream.

A shadow flicked across my face, and my eyes jerked fearfully toward the sky. A huge bird of prey wheeled and soared above me, swooped downward, its unblinking eyes seeming to pierce my soul before it sailed from sight like my *Ka* would when I died. I shivered and ran from the place.

An hour later I was still pacing the floor, trying to collect what remained of my thoughts. I was an American in a modern Egyptian hotel. My woman was in the same place. But was she my woman? Another woman had once shown the same look of fear and distrust as she looked at me; she had run away and never returned. I ran across the room and grabbed the phone.

"Miss Barkley's room!" I ordered.

A voice said, "I am sorry, M. Andrews. I believe Miss Barkley received a call and left ten minutes ago."

I replaced the phone and stood, staring down at it. Durand, probably the only man in Egypt who knew her, must have called. Things were not falling right; they had to be gathered up and worked over. My star was rising in the heavens, and it was too early for it to become cinders.

I went to the bar and got drunk.

The ringing of the phone awakened me early the next morning, hammering at my ears and playing a fiendish tune on my temples. I reached for the receiver weakly and picked it up. "Hello," I muttered. "What is it?"

"Janice," the voice replied softly.

As quickly as I could I sat up, lit a cigarette and shuddered as the smoke reaching my lungs. "Hello," I said. "How are you this wonderful morning?" I asked her gently.

"I called to say goodbye," she replied.

My stomach dropped and the walls appeared to fall in on me. "Goodbye!" I cried. "Where are you going?"

Her voice returned in a rush, "I know more than I did yesterday," she said. "I might have been willing to discount what the old man said as the ravings of a madman. But now I know better."

I hated to hear the answer, but I said, "What do you mean?"

"You—killed my father." Her voice was very calm.

My breath ended up something like a shudder. "I know you did, Rolly, because I saw the clothes he wore last night. The medicine was in his left pocket. You see—he always carried it in the right pocket, he could reach it easier that way.

"He was left-handed, Rolly!"

"Janice!" I shouted. "I have to talk with you!"

"It's no use, I am calling from the airport. In a few minutes I will be leaving. I just wanted you to know that at least a part of the old man's prophecy is coming true."

There was a booming of the loudspeaker, a short silence, then two final words, "Goodbye, Rolly."

A small sob, a click, then nothing.

The phone dropped from my hand, I got sick and ran to the bathroom. After a shower, I bounced back somewhat, but I was no more than an empty husk. She was gone, and I was here. At the window I looked up at old Cheops and hated it. After four cups of coffee I felt more like a complete man, and as my cigarette smouldered in the ash tray, things became clear, like the water in the goblet.

I would re-enter the tomb, taking up where David Barkley had left off. But instead of grabbing the glory for myself, I would see that he received it. I would not let Durand mention my name, because now fame meant less than nothing to me, it had taken on a negative quality. I left hurriedly for the lobby, preparing to go into town, pick up tools, then revisit the tomb and try to pick up the pieces of my life which lay scattered somewhere down there.

"M. Andrews, may I speak with you, please?" It was the desk clerk, and I turned and walked back. "M. Durand has been trying to reach you for the last hour. You were not in your room, so I presumed you had left the grounds."

"I was in the dining room," I mumbled.

"I am truly sorry," he smiled. "Durand's call was last made five minutes past." I nodded and started to pick up the house phone when he continued, "... And Miss Barkley left these articles for you—and this letter when she departed."

He handed me the letter, then pulled Barkley's bag of tools out from beneath the counter. To me it was inconceivable that Janice could be capable of such irony. It was superb!

"Shall I have them taken to your room, M. Andrews?"

I touched the crowbar. "No," I said suddenly. "I'll take them with me."

"... And if M. Durand calls again?"

"If he calls, you may tell him that I am leaving his precious Egypt soon, but first I have a debt to pay." I must have sounded a bit dramatic, because he stared at me, shrugged a Continental shoulder and turned away.

I left the burning heat of the noonday sun and descended into the musty darkness of the tomb. The damp odor swirled about me, dug its tendrils into my nostrils and clothes. I carefully placed the flashlight on the coffin, took out the tools and went to work. The coffin moved easier as I pumped the handle of the hydraulic jack back and forth. "I'm sorry, David," I said more or less to myself. It was more of a silent prayer, but I seemed to hear him say, "It's all right, boy. Just get down there into the queen's bedroom and let the world know of our discovery..."

When the coffin had slipped to one side I pried up the slab, let it come to rest against the side, then reached eagerly for the flashlight. As if possessed by some perverse demon it crashed to the floor, plunging the tomb into darkness as the light shattered. I cursed, searched the bag for one of the candles, then lit it and turned my attention to the dark chamber at my feet.

I shielded my eyes from the light, saw that there was enough unused space for a leap, then jumped down. Eerie shadows danced about me as I felt the jar as my feet hit the hard rock. My heart danced as I realized that I was the only man who had been here for eras that were dead and forgotten centuries before Christ was born.

Queen Hetepheres was lying in state, her body encased in a golden likeness, her painted eyes carrying a look of supreme secrecy. Boxes and caskets of gold were within her easy reach. I touched one and as I raised the top, the hinges fell apart. I smiled, thinking how David would have enjoyed this moment, and ran my finger through the rougue which was supposed one day to re-adorn her face when she was called upon to face Osiris.

I turned to wipe my discolored finger on the wall when I saw what David had been searching for. Next to me were painted inscriptions on the wall, tracing the missing generation which had suffered oblivion for thousands of generations.

I bumped into a half-upright mummy case and barely caught it before it fell onto the next one. Three slaves had been placed there to protect her from the likes of me, and the poor devils who had died in terror would never know it had all been in vain.

From across the chamber, a sparkle caught my eye. A small casket was begging for attention. I walked toward it, removed the lid, then dipped my hands inside and cupped a handful of uncut diamonds and rubies. As they trickled through my fingers and fell to the floor I laughed softly. I would not have given a dime for the whole mess of them.

The candle flickered to a new low, then sputtered and died completely. At the same instant I reeled and stumbled to my knees, my lungs trying to get air which was not there. As I fell to the floor on my face, my half-conscious mind screamed that I should have realized that after the countless eras of being sealed up the air would be heavy and unpure, and the lighter air from above could not filter down.

I tried to hoist myself up, my legs kicking frantically to get a hold on her mummy case. Once they did, and my mouth was level with the floor of the tomb. I got three huge gulps of good air, then slipped and fell to the floor of her chamber. I lay on my back, staring upward. The weak shaft of light from far above slanted diagonally across the wall of the queen's chamber. Then suddenly a stronger light shot down blindly, and a voice followed shouting something that lost its meaning in the echoing of the tomb.

Three times I tried to return its call, but my lips moved soundlessly. Then the light withdrew. I forced myself erect and climbed onto the mummy case again. When I forced myself to climb to the main floor, I saw a small square of natural light. I patted it, and felt like bending forward to kiss it. Then in tune with a grating noise from above, the light grew smaller, a foot, then less, and my hand clawed at it, an inch, then nothing but complete blackness as the slab once again covered the hole far above me.

For hours I sat in the darkness. Once I screamed, but there was only one answer—my own voice echoing back from the distant shore of insanity. When I tried to think rationally, it was no good, because thinking can go only so far when you constantly reach a dead end on every thought.

Then I recalled the letter Janice had written. I lit the candle again and jerked the letter from my pocket.

"Dear Rolly, I am leaving. Once I thought I loved you, but now I cannot. As surely as if you had stabbed him, you killed my father. I am not going to the police, this is between you and your God, if you have one. I have directed M. Durand to reseal the tomb. From the way you talked to him, and your eagerness to explore it further, he believes there may have been a discovery. But he is following my wishes and will not re-open the tomb until next spring. Goodbye.

Janice.

THE END

www.ingramcontent.com/pod-product-compliance
Lightning Source LLC
Chambersburg PA
CBHW030545200626
46808CB00025BA/3053